Grandpa's Angel

Jutta Bauer

Grandpa's Angel

CANDLEWICK PRESS
CAMBRIDGE, MASSACHUSETTS

Grandpa loved telling stories.

He told me stories whenever I went to visit him. . . .

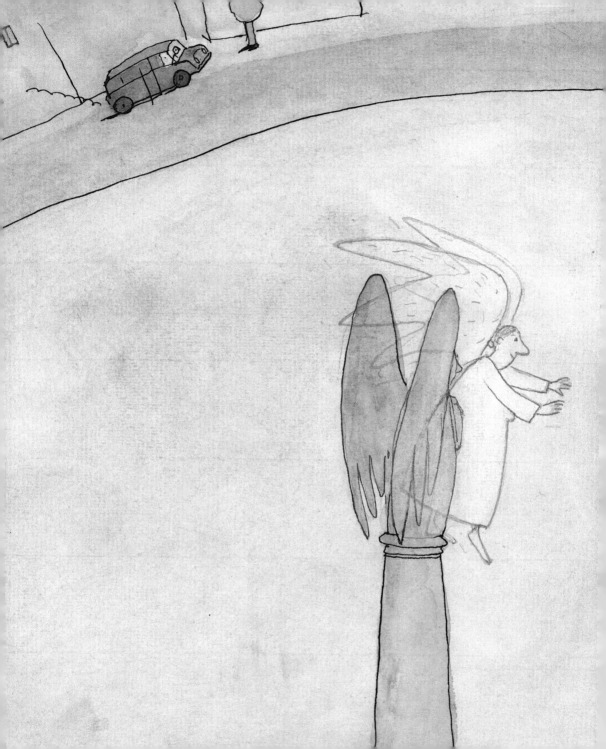

"Every morning on my way to school, I ran through the town square.

In the middle of the square stood a large statue
of an angel. I never stopped to look at it. I was
always rushing, and my book bag was heavy.

Once I was almost run over by a bus . . .

even though back then, there wasn't much traffic.

It was a long walk to school. There were holes in the ground . . .

lonely street corners . . .

and some pretty scary geese.

But I wasn't afraid. I was always the bravest.
I climbed the highest trees . . .

and dove into the deepest lakes.

Big dogs trembled in front of me.

I had enemies, and I fought them.
Sometimes I lost . . .

but not too often.

I was never a coward, although I didn't
know how dangerous times were back then.

My friend Joseph knew. He was frightened.
One day, he disappeared.
I never saw him again, which made me very sad.

I was slowly growing up . . .

but life wasn't getting any easier.

There was war . . .

and hunger . . .

I took whatever
work I could get . . .

even if I wasn't very good at it.

I fell in love . . .

became a father . . .

built a house . . .

bought a car . . .

and became a grandfather.

All in all, it's been a beautiful life . . .

even if at times a little strange.

I've been very lucky."

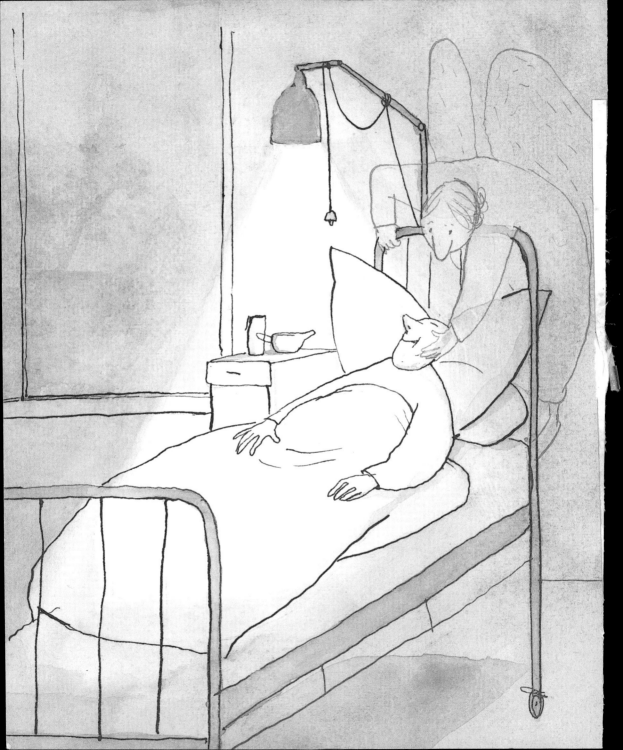

Grandpa was tired and closed his eyes.
I left quietly.

Outside, it was still clear and warm.
What a beautiful day!

Copyright © 2001 by CARLSEN Verlag GmbH, Hamburg, Germany
First published in Germany under the title OPAS ENGEL

This edition published by arrangement with CARLSEN Verlag GmbH, Hamburg, Germany

English translation copyright © 2005 by Walker Books Ltd., London, England

First U.S. edition 2005

Library of Congress Cataloging-in-Publication Data

Bauer, Jutta.
[Opas Engel. German]
Grandpa's angel / Jutta Bauer. — 1st U.S. ed.
p. cm.
Summary: An elderly man shares his life story with his grandson, complete with long, dangerous walks to
school, war, love and marriage, and a very special protector.
ISBN 0-7636-2743-7
[1. Angels — Fiction. 2. Grandfathers — Fiction.] I. Title.
PZ7.B32617Gr 2005
[E] — dc22   2004057038

2 4 6 8 10 9 7 5 3 1

Printed in China

This book was typeset in JansonText and Univers and hand lettered by the author.
The illustrations were done in gouache and ink

Candlewick Press
2067 Massachusetts Avenue
Cambridge, Massachusetts 02140

visit us at www.candlewick.com